Curious George®

Fire Dog Rescue

Adaptation by Julie Tibbott
Based on the TV series teleplay written by Scott Gray

Houghton Mifflin Harcourt
Boston New York

For information about permission to reproduce selections from this book, write to Permissions, Houghton Mifflin Harcourt Publishing Company, 215 Park Avenue South, New York, New York 10003.

ISBN: 978-0-544-50202-4 paper-over-board
ISBN: 978-0-544-50320-5 paperback

Design by Afsoon Razavi

www.hmhco.com

Printed in China
SCP 10 9 8 7 6 5 4 3 2 1
4500530037

AGES	GRADES	GUIDED READING LEVEL	READING RECOVERY LEVEL	LEXILE ® LEVEL
5-7	1	J	17	440L

One day, George walked past the firehouse.
A dog ran out!
He was friendly.
He wanted to play ball with George.

There were two new friends at the fire
station.
Sam was training to be a firefighter. He was
also in charge of the new fire dog, Blaze.

Sam brought Blaze inside and George
headed home.
But he had a strange feeling he was being
followed.

Suddenly, Sam was calling him.
"George! Blaze followed you out of the
station. I have to keep him safe to pass
my firefighter test, but he keeps running
away."

Sam was in trouble.
What if he had not found Blaze?
How would someone know to bring him
back to the firehouse?

When Sam went to train, George stayed
with Blaze.
He had an idea. Everything in the station
had a label with the station number on it.

Maybe Blaze needed a label too!
After a little searching, George found a
firehouse label.
He didn't even make that big of a mess . . .

Well, for a monkey!
George put the label on Blaze.
Now everyone would know where
Blaze belonged.

On his way home,
George passed Betsy, Steve, and Charkie
playing in the park . . . with Blaze!

Blaze was on the run again!
Sam wasn't far behind.
"He went that way!" Steve and Betsy said,
pointing in different directions.

George knew a way to find Blaze.
He climbed the nearest tree for a better
view.
Uh-oh! George saw Blaze going into a truck.

"They took Blaze!" Sam cried.
"That's the animal shelter truck," Betsy
said. "He'll be safe there. Shelters take
care of lost pets."

Sam and George rushed to the animal
shelter. The shelter worker took them
to the kennel. Blaze was safe—and very
excited to see them!

But Blaze didn't want to say goodbye to his new friend at the shelter. Now George knew why Blaze kept running away. He was lonely!

They brought Blaze and his new friend back to the firehouse.
"George figured out how to stop Blaze from running away," said Sam. "Meet Sparky!"

"The shelter worker said some dogs do better with a friend," Sam said. "And they should always wear collars showing their name, address, and phone number."

"Now, let's go take that firefighter test. I'm ready! Both dogs will be here when we're done . . . right, George?"

Sam did great on his firefighter test.
He finished the obstacle course in less
than two minutes!

"Good job!" the other firefighters said.
"But you still need to pass the other test.
We have to see if the dogs are still in the
firehouse."

Success! Sam passed both his tests. He would get to be a firefighter after all. And it was all thanks to a little help from a monkey.

What Do Fire Dogs Do?

Most dogs that help firefighters are white dogs with black spots called Dalmatians, like Blaze.

The Dalmatian is very strong, and can run long distances without getting tired. Those are important skills to have when helping to fight fires!

Dalmatians also have a calming effect on horses, which was helpful back in the days before fire trucks, when horse-drawn fire wagons were used.

A fire dog guards the firehouse. On the scene of a fire, the dog guards the fire truck while the firefighters are working to put out the blaze.

The brave Dalmatian has also been known to rescue people from burning buildings.

Dalmatians have a lot of energy, and need to run and play. If you are willing to give your dog lots of exercise, a Dalmatian could be a good pet for you!

Here's how to draw your own Dalmatian. Use a separate piece of paper and follow the steps below.

Don't forget to add spots!

Animal Shelters Rule!

Animal shelters are great places to adopt a pet or even lend a helping hand! Here's why:

Animal shelters rescue all kinds of animals. In addition to cats and dogs, many animal shelters have rabbits, mice, birds, and guinea pigs. Some even have turtles, chickens, and reptiles, all waiting for their forever home.

If you can't have a pet at home, you may be able to volunteer with a parent or guardian at your local animal shelter. There, you can care for and play with lots of cute animals, and help them find homes.

Workers at animal shelters know the animals well. They know each animal's history, the games they like to play, and what cuddles they love best. Plus, they can teach you how to care for a pet.

There's a lot to know about pet care, but here are a few basic tips to get you started:

- Most pets should wear collars with tags that tell their name and their owner's name, address, and phone number.
- Make sure your pet has plenty of clean, fresh water, and find out what their diet and feeding schedule is.
- Every pet needs a place to call home—whether that's a tank, cage, or doghouse.
- Just like people, pets need plenty of love and attention!